Siti's Sisters

Set One
Workbook Two

Accompanies the Siti's Sisters reading books

- Odd One Out
- Taken for a Ride
- Trouble with Teachers

By Helen Bird

Ransom

Siti's Sisters Set One Workbook Two
by Helen Bird

Illustrated by Cathy Brett

Published by Ransom Publishing Ltd.
51 Southgate Street, Winchester, Hants. SO23 9EH
www.ransom.co.uk

ISBN 978 184167 646 3
First published in 2008
Copyright © 2008 Ransom Publishing Ltd.

Illustrations copyright © 2007 Cathy Brett.

Contents

Introduction

The purpose of this material is to provide opportunities to check students' understanding of the Siti's Sisters stories and to provide structures to encourage writing in a range of forms.

Students working at the reading level assumed by these books frequently have a mismatch between their experiential and oral skills and their skills in reading and writing. The Siti's Sisters stories and the support materials are intended to be:

- appealing and engaging, particularly to girls who may be otherwise reluctant to read

- age appropriate

- achievable

- appropriately challenging.

This workbook covers three of the Siti's Sisters titles, *Odd One Out*, *Taken for a Ride* and *Trouble with Teachers*. There are eight worksheets for each title, though the worksheets on diary writing and reviewing are generic and can be used for any title in the series. In each set of titles there is one worksheet that tests understanding of the events in the story, then a range of other material including formal, sentence level work and opportunities for creative writing. Rubric has been kept to a minimum on the worksheets.

Each worksheet is fully supported by teacher's notes. For these students it is essential that the work on the sheets is prepared as a class or group exercise, and suggestions for this are provided. These include oral work and shared writing. Simply handing out the worksheets, perhaps as a homework exercise, is unlikely to be successful.

Odd One Out

WORKSHEET 1:
Telling the Story – Donna's Point of View

 TASK

To retell the story. Writing in the first person.

 SUPPORT

This worksheet can be completed in stages by filling in the relevant section after reading each chapter of the story, or it can be used to review the whole book as one exercise.

If working in stages, review the chapter orally before students start writing.

EXTENSION

Choose one of the following chapters and write about the events of the chapter from that person's point of view.

Chapter Two – written from Donna's point of view.

Chapter Seven – written from Siti's point of view.

Use the model from the worksheet to help the writing.

WORKSHEET 2:
Donna's Family

TASK

To write a mini-biography of each member of Donna's family. To use context clues from the text and pictures.

SUPPORT

Read Chapters One to Four of the story. List the members of Donna's family.

Discuss what you find out about each person in the family.

If students have read other books in the series, they may have found out other facts. If so, they can add these facts to the information listed.

Write the details in the boxes on the sheet.

Alternatively, create a short biography for each of the characters and ask students to identify the character when you read out the biography.

 EXTENSION

Create a set of biography boxes for people in the student's own family, or for the student's group of friends.

Odd One Out

WORKSHEET 3:
Siti and Briony

 TASK

To write a conversation.

 SUPPORT

Note that students will need to have read all of the book before completing this task.

Read Chapter Five of the story. Discuss Donna's feelings in this chapter: Why was she crying when Siti found her? How did she feel about Marie and Briony? List some words to describe her feelings.

What did Siti plan to say to Donna? Discuss what she might have said.

What did Siti find out from Donna? What might her reaction be? Discuss how this would have changed Siti's feelings.

Review the conventions of writing direct speech. Then write the conversation where Siti tells Briony about Donna's feelings and Briony explains their plans.

 EXTENSION

Write a further conversation between Briony and Marie, where Briony tells Marie about Siti's comments.

WORKSHEET 4:
Friends

 TASK

Poetry writing.

 SUPPORT

Explain that many people like to write poetry when they are feeling unhappy. Donna is trying to cheer herself up by thinking about her friends, so she starts to write a poem.

Discuss how friends can help cheer you up when things are going wrong. List the ideas on the board.

Look at the form of the poem. Identify which of the suggestions you've listed would make sense in each stanza of the poem.

The completed poems could be illustrated and used for display.

 EXTENSION

Work in pairs, or as a group, to devise a questionnaire to find out if you are a good friend. Base the questions on the ideas listed earlier.

Odd One Out

WORKSHEET 5:
The Tea Party

 TASK:

Diary writing – from two different points of view.

 SUPPORT:

Read the passage on the worksheet about the tea party. Then look at the picture.

Why did Donna feel that the party was just as awful as she had anticipated? What things about the party would you describe as childish?

How did Donna feel? Make a list of useful words to describe her feelings.

How do you think the rest of the girls felt? Remember that, by this time, they knew that Donna's sisters had planned something special. Kelly had gone with Siti to talk to Briony. How do you think Kelly felt during the tea party? Make a list of useful words to describe her feelings.

Following the discussion, ask students to make notes, on the worksheet, for diary entries for Donna and Kelly. Finally choose one of the two girls and write a longer diary entry using the generic diary page.

 EXTENSION:

Role-play a conversation between Donna and her mum, where Donna says 'thank you' for the party but tries, tactfully, to suggest that jelly and cakes weren't really what she wanted. Turn this role-play into a play script.

WORKSHEET 6:
A Surprise Birthday Party

 TASK:

To complete a checklist to plan a party.

 SUPPORT:

One of the most important aspects of party planning is choosing the venue. Most parties are held at home. Discuss how you would persuade parents to:

a) allow you to have a party
b) go out for the evening.

Who would help you organise the party? Discuss appropriate food. (Would you buy in pizzas or cook food, or just provide crisps etc.?) Discuss what you would provide for entertainment. Discuss the cost of a party.

Think about things that could go wrong. List these and decide what you could do to prevent a disaster.

ICT opportunity: design invitations to your party. These could include reply slips. Use these invitations for display.

 EXTENSION:

Use the same planning sheet to plan a party for a much younger child – e.g. a sibling or younger cousin.

Odd One Out

WORKSHEET 7:
Planning a Story 1

❤ TASK:

Story planning: looking at characters.

This worksheet is best used together with Worksheet 8: *Planning a Story 2* to provide a broader story-planning activity.

❤ SUPPORT

Look at the author's 'to do' list on the worksheet. Make notes about each of the characters listed. Relate this to the work done on Worksheet 2: *Donna's Family*, where students are asked to write a mini-biography of members of Donna's family.

Discuss why the author might start by producing biographies like this.

❤ EXTENSION

Students should work through the planning exercise on the worksheet either by basing their work on the story *Odd One Out*, or they can choose a new situation from those listed and plan a book of their own. In either case, the next worksheet (Worksheet 8: *Planning a Story 2*) can be used to support and extend the activity.

WORKSHEET 8:
Planning a Story 2

❤ TASK

Story planning: thinking about plot.

❤ SUPPORT

This activity follows on from Worksheet 7: *Planning a Story 1*.

If students chose to work on a new story, they can decide on the scenario. Discuss how each of the characters would react in the situation. Note these possible responses on the sheet. Discuss and make notes about possible endings for the story.

If students chose to work on the story *Odd One Out*, they should make some guesses about the reactions and thoughts of those characters who do not play a very big part in the story. Ask students to suggest ideas for an alternative ending. This could be, for example, a different surprise for Donna.

❤ EXTENSION

Either plan further chapters for the book or work in pairs or as a whole group to write a complete chapter. If working on the story of the book, write an alternative ending.

Odd One Out

Write notes about what happens in each chapter, from Donna's point of view.

Chapter One

I walked to school with _____ . We talked about _____ .

That evening, my mum said _____

_____ .

Chapter Two

I told Briony, Marie and Michael about _____

Briony said _____ . Marie said _____

Michael said _____ . Mum saw that I _____ .

She said _____ . The problem is _____

_____ .

Chapter Three

I told Siti about _____ .

At home, Marie and Briony _____ .

Chapter Four

When I tried to talk to Marie and Briony, they _____

Dad said _____ . I felt _____ .

Marie and Briony kept _____

Chapter Five

I felt _____ . When Siti found me, I was _____ .

She said _____ .

Chapter Six

It was my _____ . I noticed that the Sisters _____ .

After school _____ .

Chapter Seven

The tea party was _____ On Saturday we all went _____ .

Afterwards _____ . I felt _____ .

But then _____ .

We went _____ . I felt _____ .

Siti's Sisters

Odd One Out

What do we find out about the people in Donna's family? Fill in the biography boxes.

Marie is Donna's

Briony is

Donna's Mum

Donna's Dad

Michael is

Siti's Sisters

Odd One Out

Siti found Donna in tears. This is what she said to Kelly:

> "We've got to do something for Donna. I'm going to talk to Briony and you've got to help me."

Siti found out that Briony and Marie were secretly planning a birthday barbecue. They didn't want Donna to find out! Briony made Siti promise not to tell.

Write the conversation between Briony and Siti.

Siti met Briony as she was coming out of college.

"Hi, Siti," said Briony. "You're looking serious! What's the problem?"
"Well," said Siti. "It's Donna."

_____ asked Briony.

_____ said Siti.

_____

_____

_____

_____

_____

_____

_____

Siti's Sisters

Odd One Out

Donna started to write a poem about her friends, but she got stuck!
Can you help her fill in the gaps?

Friends

Friends are important
A good friend will always

Friends are great to have.
A good friend will never

Friends are always there
When

Friends are precious!
So always remember

So when you're feeling
Find your very best friend and

Friends!

Siti's Sisters

Odd One Out

The tea party had been just as awful as Donna thought. O.K. Mum had tried her best to make it look pretty, but JELLY! Who in their right mind would give jelly and ice cream to a fourteen year old?

The Sisters had been great though. They pretended that they were having fun, but Donna knew they weren't really.

Writing about the tea party…

Make notes here to write Donna's Diary.

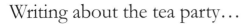

Donna's Diary

Make notes here to write Kelly's Diary.

Kelly's Diary

Siti's Sisters

Odd One Out

You are going to plan a surprise party for a best friend. Fill in the checklist:

A Surprise Birthday Party!

A party for

Age

Where?

Who's coming?

Food List

Entertainment

Things that could go wrong!

14

Siti's Sisters

Odd One Out

Characters:

Siti _____

_____

_____

_____

Donna _____

_____

_____

Kelly _____

_____

_____

Lu _____

_____

_____

Rachel _____

_____

_____

'To do' list:

1 Write a mini biography for each character – looks, family, likes and dislikes.

2 Decide who will be the main character in the story.

3 Decide what the story will be about.

Ideas for stories:

● One of the girls thinks the others don't like her any more.

● One of the girls gets a new boyfriend – but the others don't like him.

● One girl has a big row with her parents and says she is going to run away from home.

Siti's Sisters

15

Odd One Out

A title for the story _____

Chapter Notes: Chapter One – setting the scene

What is the problem? _____

What does each member of the group think?

Siti thinks _____

Rachel thinks _____

Lu thinks _____

Donna thinks _____

Kelly thinks _____

What happens next? _____

_____

What does each person say or do? _____

_____

How will your story end?

A happy ending would be

_____

_____

_____

_____

A sad ending would be

_____

_____

_____

_____

Siti's Sisters

Taken For a Ride

WORSHEET 1:
How Much Do You Remember?
Writing a Quiz

 TASK:

To check understanding of the story. To provide the correct answers and to suggest alternative answers to complete the quiz.

SUPPORT:

Check that students have understood the story. Work through the questions on the worksheet orally and establish the correct answer for each one. Write in the correct answer on one of the lines (note that this does not need to be a complete sentence).

Then work through the questions again to plan two alternative answers for each question. The alternatives are then filled in the appropriate boxes.

The completed quizzes could be used for display work or may be used as a real quiz page for a different group.

EXTENSION:

Devise and write further questions in the same format.

WORKSHEET 2:
Lu's Parents

TASK:

Looking at attitudes to parents.

SUPPORT:

Read the extracts from the text. Discuss Lu's perception of her parents. Why are her parents behaving in the way they are? What do they want for Lu?

Look at the comments on the worksheet. Discuss the sorts of things students say about their parents, or other significant adults. Why do adults always think they know best? Do they?

Decide whether Lu's comments about her parents are true. Look through the text to see if you can find evidence to support her comments.

EXTENSION:

Make a list of things that parents do to annoy their children.

Make another list of things that parents do to help and support their children.

Create a display on the good and bad things about parents, based on these lists.

Taken For a Ride

WORKSHEET 3:
Captions

TASK:

To identify the part of the story illustrated and write appropriate captions.

SUPPORT:

Review Chapters Three and Four of the story.

Identify the scenes that are illustrated in each case. Discuss what each picture tells the reader. Then complete the captions for each picture.

EXTENSION:

Continue the story in the same form. Students could either draw appropriate pictures or use pictures from other sources.

WORKSHEET 4:
Talking to Mrs Samways – Writing a Play

TASK:

To write a playscript.

SUPPORT:

Discuss why Siti says they need to go and talk to Mrs Samways.

How will they explain to Mrs Samways that Donna isn't Lu? How will they explain why Donna is pretending to be Lu? What will Mrs Samway's reaction be? What can Siti say to help the situation?

Review the conventions of script writing.

It may be helpful to students to role-play the situation before they begin the writing.

EXTENSION:

Write another section of the story – e.g. the last chapter – as a playscript, extending the existing dialogue.

WORKSHEET 5:
Open Day

 TASK:

To plan and write a newspaper report about the open day.

 SUPPORT:

Make notes in the reporter's notebook to answer the questions.

If appropriate, provide additional information about horses and competitions to enable students to answer in greater detail. This section could be done as a paired activity.

Use these notes to write a paragraph about the riding school and about 'Lu'.

Students could also use information from the book illustrations – e.g. a description of 'Lu'.

 EXTENSION:

Mrs Samways has also asked the local T.V. station to cover the event. Prepare a set of notes for her to use in a T.V. interview. This should include information about the riding school: where it is, the cost of lessons, etc. and also about her plans to turn 'Lu' into a top rider.

WORKSHEET 6:
What Happened Downstairs

 TASK:

To write an extra chapter.

 SUPPORT:

Review Chapter Seven. Identify the sequence of events. Then complete the list on the worksheet. Discuss what Lu's dad's reaction is likely to be.

What facts might have led her parents to be less cross?

Why is the situation resolved so easily? Would you have expected her parents to have been cross for longer?

What might Mrs Samways have said to help calm things down?

 EXTENSION:

Use the extra chapter to perform an improvised play.

Taken For a Ride

WORSHEET 7:
Story Plan

♥ **TASK:**

To make notes for a story based on *Taken for a Ride*.

♥ **SUPPORT:**

This is quite a challenging activity. Less able students could work on providing a plan for *Taken for a Ride*.

Alternatively, the activity could be undertaken as a group activity.

Discuss the sorts of things parents might insist you do – e.g. visiting elderly relatives on a regular basis, doing household chores in return for pocket money, going on a family holiday when you want to go with friends, looking after younger siblings.

Think about excuses for not doing the task. List these. Decide which excuses are sensible and which are silly. Could some of the sillier ideas work in the context of a story?

Decide which of the ideas might achieve the required outcome.

What are the weaknesses of your plan? What sorts of things might go wrong?

Will the other people involved forgive you? What can you say to make them more sympathetic to your point of view?

♥ **EXTENSION:**

Use the notes and write part or all of the story. If you have done the work as a group exercise, ask students to work in pairs with each pair writing one part, or chapter, of the story. Then put these together to create a whole book.

ICT opportunity: This task could be undertaken on the computer to make the production of a final piece easier.

WORKSHEET 8:
Fair or Unfair?

♥ **TASK:**

To look at a situation from more than one point of view.

♥ **SUPPORT:**

Discuss Lu's reaction to the news that she is to have riding lessons. Are her parents really doing what they think is in her best interests? Ask students whether they think she and Donna were right to do what they did? How much say do you expect to have in what your parents choose to give you?

Is the situation appropriate for punishment?

Is the punishment appropriate?

Students should then complete the sheet, giving a reason for their view on whether or not Lu should have been punished.

♥ **EXTENSION:**

Little children often say "It's not fair".

Make a list of prohibitions for toddlers, such as – don't play near the fire, don't go out of the house, stay close to mummy in the shops, you mustn't take other people's toys, etc.

Discuss these and other possibilities, and list them. Now think about the reasons underlying these prohibitions.

Create a safety poster based on your discussions.

Taken For a Ride

Why was Lu upset when she met Donna?

A _____

B _____

C _____

Why was Donna jealous?

A _____

B _____

C _____

The Sisters came up with some ideas to help Lu. What was the silly idea?

A _____

B _____

C _____

What was the sensible idea?

A _____

B _____

C _____

What made it possible to carry out their plan?

A _____

B _____

C _____

How did Lu's parents find out what the Sisters were up to?

A _____

B _____

C _____

Why did Mrs Samways want Donna to talk to her parents?

A _____

B _____

C _____

What did Mrs Samways say when the Sisters explained what was going on?

A _____

B _____

C _____

What happened in the end?

A _____

B _____

C _____

Siti's Sisters

Here are some of the things Lu says about her parents:

"Can't you just tell your mum?" asked Siti.
"I tried," said Lu. "You know what she's like."

"What about your dad?"
"No. He's worse. He just tells me how lucky I am."

"It's not fair!" she told Siti. "She doesn't listen to anything I say."

"Mum and Dad should have listened to me in the first place."

Here are some things Lu and her friends might have said about Lu's parents.

Lu said her parents	True or False?	Evidence from the story
never listen		
are unkind		
aren't interested		
don't care		
make too much fuss		
are mean		
are too bossy		
won't ever let her do what she wants		

22

Taken For a Ride

These four pictures come from the middle of the story.
Write a caption for each picture to explain what is happening.

Lu's mum is about to take Lu to the stables when _____

_____

_____

_____

_____

_____

_____

Lu rings _____

_____

_____

_____

Donna was really excited but

_____

_____

_____

_____

When they got to the stables

_____

_____

_____

_____

_____

Siti's Sisters

Taken For a Ride

Lu, Donna and Siti go and see Mrs Samways.

MRS SAMWAYS (Looking pleased)
What did your mum and dad say?
(Donna bursts into tears.)

MRS SAMWAYS
Come inside and tell me all about it.

SCENE 1

Lu, Donna and Siti go and see Mrs Samways

SITI _____

_____

MRS SAMWAYS _____

_____

DONNA _____

_____

MRS SAMWAYS _____

_____

SITI _____

_____

MRS SAMWAYS _____

_____

DONNA _____

_____

SITI _____

_____

MRS SAMWAYS I'm sorry, my dears. I just can't do it. (She turns to Lu.)
If I were your mum I'd want the truth. (She turns to Donna.)
But I don't want you to have to give up. Is there any chance...

DONNA (Interrupting) No way. We just can't afford it.

24

Siti's Sisters

Reporter's notebook — Riding school open day: Saturday

Questions to ask:

Owner's name

What's being shown during open day?

What do you need to know to be a rider?

What other jobs do you need to do in a riding school?

Do you need lots of lessons to be a champion?

Who is your best rider?

What are your plans for that person?

Open day at the riding school

Saturday saw an open day at the riding school.
The owner, Mrs Samways, said that

"Lu Clarke – the best rider we've ever had."

Siti's Sisters

Lu's mum has seen the paper! Lu is sent upstairs to her room.

Complete this list of what happened downstairs.

Lu's father comes home.

Lu's mum tells him _____

_____

Lu's father rings _____

She says that _____

_____

Lu's father also rings _____

They _____

Use these notes to help you finish this extra chapter for the story. It will be about what happens downstairs.

When Mr Clarke arrives home, he finds Mrs Clark looking annoyed.
"What's happened?" he asks.
"It's Lu! You'll never guess what she's been doing every Saturday!
She _____

_____

_____

_____

_____

_____

_____

Siti's Sisters

Taken For a Ride

Like Lu, sometimes there are things in life you really don't want to do!
Plan your own story using this idea.

Story Plan

You find out about the thing you don't want to do. What is it?

Who is making you do it?

You make a list of possible ways to get out of it.

You decide on your plan.

You carry out your plan!

Something goes wrong and you are found out.

Everything works out O.K. in the end.

Siti's Sisters

Lu's dad says

"And you can go too. Your punishment is to go and be a stable girl for a term. Mrs Samways has a really big shovel for mucking out!"

Should Lu have been punished or not?

List the reasons why she **should** have been punished.	List the reasons why she **shouldn't** have been punished.
A	A
B	B
C	C

What do you think?

I think Lu's punishment was fair   unfair

because _____

_____

_____

_____

_____

_____

_____

Siti's Sisters

Trouble with Teachers

WORKSHEET 1:
Reading and Understanding

❤ **TASK:**

Comprehension – demonstrating understanding of the text.

❤ **SUPPORT:**

Identify the section of each chapter where students will be able to find the answer to each question on the worksheet.

Encourage students to write their answers in complete sentences.

❤ **EXTENSION:**

Devise a similar sheet with students. Work on one new question for each chapter. Do the task in pairs, and then swap sheets for the rest of the group to answer the new questions.

WORKSHEET 2:
Mapping the Story

❤ **TASK:**

Identify where in the school the various events in the story took place. List these events in numerical order.

❤ **SUPPORT:**

Discuss the part of the school shown on the map. The answer to the first location has been given as an example.

❤ **EXTENSION:**

Discuss Lola's timetable for the day. Draw up a timetable for a visiting author to your school. Identify what types of books an author might write. Discuss what the author might talk about. What types of books would be most interesting to what sorts of groups?

WORKSHEET 3:
Visitors

 TASK:

Draw up a list of *Dos and Don'ts* for looking after an important visitor to your school.

 SUPPORT:

Discuss what Mrs Williams might have said to Rachel and Lu. What is 'the same old stuff'? Why do schools want to impress visitors?

List examples of good behaviour.

Discuss the sorts of things a school might like to keep hidden from visitors. List examples of this type of behaviour.

Choose the most appropriate to list on the worksheet in the form of a poster.

 EXTENSION:

Discuss and list some appropriate school rules to ensure good behaviour. These could be rules for the whole school or just for behaviour in your classroom.

WORKSHEET 4:
Lola's Point of View

 TASK:

Writing from a different viewpoint.

 SUPPORT:

List the events of Chapters Four and Five up to the point when they reach the classroom. You may like to refer to the information collected on Worksheet 2 *Mapping the Story*. Write a detailed ending for each of the sentence starts on the sheet.

Discuss what Lola's response to the events might have been. Was she amused or cross? Did she realise what the girls were trying to do?

 EXTENSION:

Choose one of the Sisters and write some notes about her, as Lola might write them. Look at the pictures in the book and try to include information about the girl which includes what Lola would *see*, as well as what they might say to her.

WORKSHEET 5:
Thoughts

 TASK:

To devise additional text in the form of speech bubbles.

 SUPPORT:

Students will first have to work out where the incidents in the pictures occur in the story, and identify which character is doing the thinking (i.e. has the speech bubble attached).

The illustrations are from page 24 (Siti), page 27 (Lola), page 33 (Siti) and page 35 (Mrs Williams).

Discuss the situation in each case; then ask students to devise a sentence to sum up the probable thoughts of each of the characters at that point.

 EXTENSION:

Ask students to select another picture from the book and devise an appropriate thought bubble for one of the characters.

WORKSHEET 6:
Explanation

 TASK:

To write an explanation text.

 SUPPORT:

Discuss what Mrs Williams would have thought when she found out that Lola had been locked in the ICT room. Add to the Word Bank appropriate words which could be used to describe her feelings.

Why did she think it was the Sisters' fault?

Discuss her feelings when she got back to the staffroom and heard what Lola had to say. Add to the Word Bank more words that you could use to describe her feelings at this point.

Do you think that Mrs Williams would have found it as funny as Lola did?

 EXTENSION:

Write a letter from Mrs Williams to Lola to thank her for coming and apologising for all the problems.

WORKSHEET 7:
Newspaper Report

 TASK:

Writing in a different format.

 SUPPORT:

Go through the questions on the worksheet and discuss appropriate notes to make.

Ask students to back up their answers with evidence from the text, where possible.

This could be done as a role-play exercise. If the story is not sufficiently clear on all the points, make up appropriate information.

Discuss the merits of having writers visiting schools. Would the group like to have such a visit?

 EXTENSION:

Write a newspaper article based on the information compiled in the exercise. This could be undertaken as an ICT task. The completed newspaper articles could be used for display purposes.

WORKSHEET 8:
Visiting Writer

 TASK:

To write a letter to invite an author into school. Prepare questions to ask a visiting writer.

 SUPPORT:

Review the conventions of letter writing. Then plan the letter to Lola Leigh. The letter might suggest dates for a visit. Include information about your school and why Lola would enjoy visiting you. Say that you like reading her books.

Finally, discuss what the group would like to find out about an author. The questions could be written for Lola Leigh, but it might be more interesting for students to prepare questions for a well-known author, possibly an author of a book they have read.

 EXTENSION:

Plan and produce a poster inviting parents into school for a talk by your author.

Can you answer these questions?

Why did Kelly especially want to meet Lola Leigh?

_____

_____

What did Mrs Williams think was important?

_____

_____

Why did Kelly pull a face?

_____

_____

Why did Siti suddenly change direction?

_____

_____

Why didn't Mrs Williams look pleased?

_____

_____

Why didn't Siti think what had happened was the Sisters' fault?

_____

_____

Why was Mrs Williams interested instead of cross?

_____

_____

Siti's Sisters

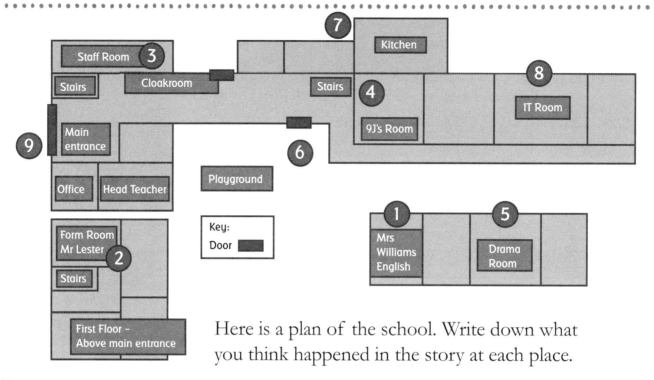

Here is a plan of the school. Write down what you think happened in the story at each place.

1. They were at school early. They went to see Mrs Williams so she could tell them what to do.

2.

3.

4.

5.

6.

7.

8.

9.

Trouble with Teachers

What did Mrs Williams say to Rachel and Lu about looking after the visitor?

_____

_____

Things you should do when we have a visitor.

Things you should never do when we have a visitor.

Siti's Sisters

Trouble with Teachers

Lola likes to collect ideas for her books. She makes notes about things that happen to her. This is part of the day from Lola's point of view.

Five girls came to collect me from the staff room, though I only expected two of them! They told me that the drama studio was on the other side of the school, so we all set off together. A polite girl called Rachel talked to me on the way. Then something strange happened.

We had just reached the door to the playground when

I think the girls must have been worried that

We reached the school cloakroom when

One of the girls said

After a short wait, we all

One of the girls got to the corner of the building when, for some reason,

I was beginning to wonder

I asked

We turned around and

We got to the classroom at last. The teacher

Siti's Sisters

Trouble with Teachers

These four pictures come from different parts of the story.

Work out what is happening in each picture, then fill in the thought bubble.

Siti's Sisters

Trouble with Teachers

Siti's dad, Mr Musa, is a senior teacher at the school. He wasn't pleased when he heard that the school's visiting writer got locked in the computer room by mistake! He asked Mrs Williams to write him a note to explain how it had happened. What did she say?

Word Bank

angry   funny
upset   laughing
worried

Here is her note:

> I had started my afternoon lesson when a message came from
>
> 9F to let me know that Ms Leigh hadn't arrived for their lesson.
>
> I went off to look for her. I found her _____
>
> _____
>
> By this time it was nearly _____
>
> I went to see the girls who were looking after her.
>
> They were _____
>
> _____
>
> I got them out of their lesson to _____
>
> _____
>
> When we got back to the staffroom _____
>
> _____
>
> Ms Leigh said _____
>
> _____
>
> _____

Siti's Sisters

A report of Lola's visit to the school appeared in the local paper.

You are the reporter. These are the notes you made.

Information on the writer

Name _____

What sort of books does she write? _____

What did she do during the visit?
(They wouldn't talk about things that had gone wrong!)

_____

_____

Two comments from a teacher

_____

_____

We invited her because

_____

The school gained a lot from the visit. She

_____

Two comments from students at the school

_____

_____

I liked

_____

I thought that

_____

The writer said

_____

Siti's Sisters

Trouble with Teachers

Your school would like Lola Leigh to visit. Write a letter to her to invite her to your school.

Dear Ms Leigh,

I am writing to invite you to visit our school.

Imagine a writer – not Lola – visits your school. Like Kelly, you would like to be a writer. What questions would you like to ask?

Question 1

Question 2

Question 3

Question 4

Siti's Sisters

40